FOCUS ON THE FAMILY® PRESENTS

Revenge *of the* Red Knight

BOOK 4

MARIANNE HERING • PAUL McCUSKER
ILLUSTRATED BY DAVID HOHN

TYNDALE

FOCUS ON THE FAMILY • ADVENTURES IN ODYSSEY®
TYNDALE HOUSE PUBLISHERS, INC. • CAROL STREAM, ILLINOIS

To KDH: A white knight to Russian orphans. —MKH

Revenge of the Red Knight
Copyright © 2011 Focus on the Family

A Focus on the Family book published by
Tyndale House Publishers, Inc., Carol Stream, Illinois 60188

Focus on the Family and Adventures in Odyssey, and their accompanying logos
and designs, and The Imagination Station, are federally registered trademarks of
Focus on the Family, Colorado Springs, CO 80995.

TYNDALE and Tyndale's quill logo are registered trademarks of Tyndale House
Publishers, Inc.

With the exception of known historical characters, all characters are the product
of the authors' imaginations.

Cover design by Michael Heath, Magnus Creative

Library of Congress Cataloging-in-Publication Data
Hering, Marianne.
Revenge of the Red Knight / [Marianne Hering and Paul McCusker].
    p. cm. -- (Imagination Station ; [bk. #4])
  "Focus on the Family." "Adventures in Odyssey."
Summary: Eight-year-old cousins Patrick and Beth find themselves 1450's
England during the War of the Roses, where they discover the missing treasures
and meet the person who has been sending notes through the Imagination
Station.
  ISBN 978-1-58997-630-6
  [1. Space and time--Fiction. 2. Knights and knighthood--Fiction. 3. Robbers and
outlaws--Fiction. 4. Cousins--Fiction. 5. Christian life--Fiction. 6. Great Britain-
-History--Wars of the Roses, 1455-1485--Fiction.] I. McCusker, Paul, 1958- II.
Title.
  PZ7.H431258Rev 2011
  [Fic]--dc22   2011009858

Printed in the United States of America
6 7 8 9 / 16 15 14 13

Praise for The Imagination Station® book series

These books are a great combination of history and adventure in a clean manner perfect for young readers!

—Margie B., *My Springfield Mommy* blog

Revenge of the Red Knight is an exciting mystery book . . . like the [scary] books we read in school.

—Jarod, age 8 • Papillon, Nebraska

I want to know who Albert is. I want . . . more of these books.

—Taylor, age 10 • Torrance, California

These books will help my kids enjoy history.

—Beth S., third-grade public school teacher •

Colorado Springs, Colorado

My nine-year-old son has already read [the first two books], one of them twice. He is very eager to read more in the series too. I am planning on reading them out loud to my younger son.

—Abbi C., mother of four • Minnesota

[The Imagination Station books] focus on God much more than the Magic Tree House books do.

—Emilee, age 7 • Waynesboro, Pennsylvania

Revenge *of the* Red Knight

BOOK 4

Other books in this series

Contents

Prologue

There is an old house in the town of
Odyssey. It's called Whit's End. Kids love it.
It has an ice-cream shop. It also has a lot of
rooms with games and displays.

There are exciting things to do at Whit's
End. Kids have fun and learn there.

Mr. Whittaker owns Whit's End. He is a
kind inventor. One of his inventions is the
Imagination Station.

The Imagination Station lets kids see

history in person. It's a lot like a time machine.

One day the Imagination Station broke. Mr. Whittaker didn't know why. He tried to fix the machine in his workshop.

Two cousins, Patrick and Beth, came to visit him. Patrick and Beth are eight years old.

Patrick touched the Imagination

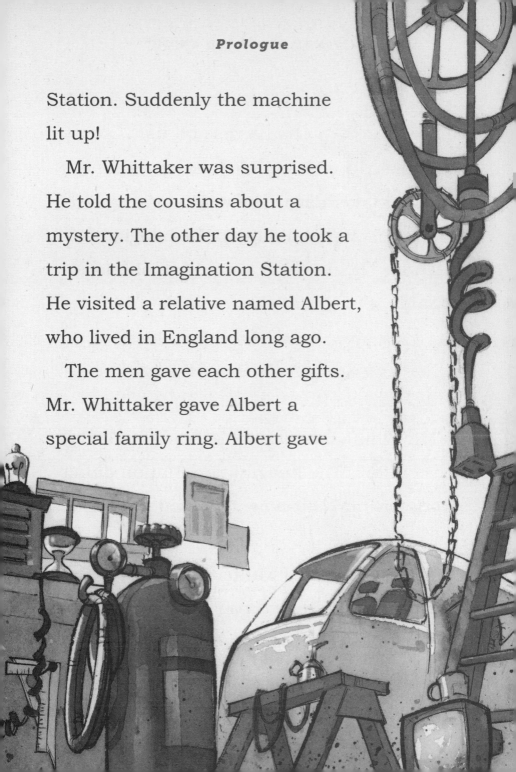

Station. Suddenly the machine lit up!

Mr. Whittaker was surprised. He told the cousins about a mystery. The other day he took a trip in the Imagination Station. He visited a relative named Albert, who lived in England long ago.

The men gave each other gifts. Mr. Whittaker gave Albert a special family ring. Albert gave

Mr. Whittaker a fancy ring. It had a rose on it.

Mr. Whittaker came home. The next morning he found a note in the Imagination Station. The note was written on old paper. It said:

To save Albert, I need a Viking Sunstone before the new moon. Or Lord Darkthorn will lock him inside the tower.

Mr. Whittaker wanted to help Albert. But he couldn't. The Imagination Station didn't work for him. But now it worked for Patrick and Beth.

The cousins also wanted to help Albert. So they traveled to Greenland. They found a Viking Sunstone.

The next day another note came. It said this:

More trouble for Albert. Lord Darkthorn is angry. The Roman monk's silver cup is missing. We need it before the new moon. May God be with you.

Again Patrick and Beth asked to help. They visited ancient Rome. The cousins found the silver cup.

A strange thing happened in Rome. An English knight arrived in the Imagination Station. The cousins were amazed. How could a knight use the Imagination Station?

The knight gave them a message:

"You must tell Mr. Whittaker to search for the golden tablet of Kublai Khan."

Beth and Patrick went on another adventure. They met Kublai Khan in China. They were given

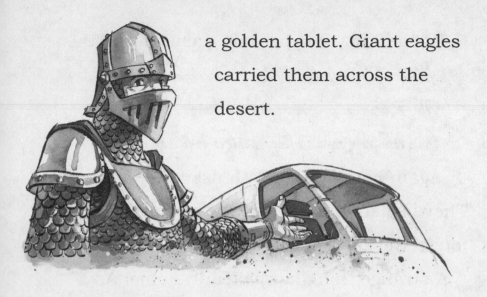

a golden tablet. Giant eagles carried them across the desert.

Then the cousins got in the Imagination Station. They tried to get back to Whit's End. But something went wrong. Patrick and Beth landed in a dark cave.

Now Patrick and Beth have a lot of questions:

What is wrong with the Imagination Station?

How will they get the golden tablet to Albert?

Where—and when—*are they?*

The cousins are about to find out.

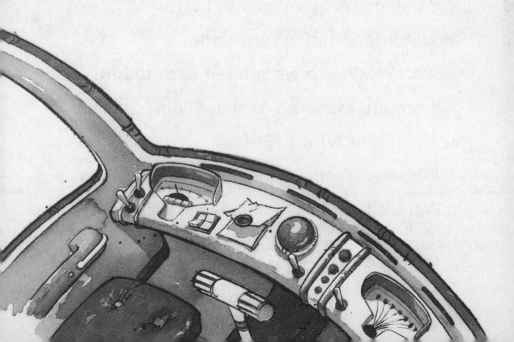

The Cave

Patrick blinked. The darkness wouldn't go away.

He stood on stony ground. The Imagination Station was gone.

"Patrick?" Beth whispered next to him. "Where are we?" she asked. "This isn't the workshop at Whit's End."

"I know," Patrick said.

Patrick heard the echo of his voice. The air around him was damp and cool. He narrowed his eyes. The darkness turned to deep blacks. Then grays. Then the blacks and grays took shape.

Patrick reached out and took a step. His fingers touched a rock wall. It was bumpy and slimy.

"We're in a cave," Patrick said.

"A cave!" Beth said. "What cave? Where is it?"

"You mean *'When is it?'* " Patrick said. "I think we jumped to another time."

"I don't care *when,*" Beth said. "I don't like caves at *any* time. What if a bear is in here?"

Patrick didn't like that thought.

He looked around. Beth was still clutching the golden tablet. It seemed to glow in the dull light.

He heard a rustling sound above him. He looked up and squinted. Something was moving around on the ceiling.

"Bats," he whispered.

Beth groaned and said, "I hate bats as much as I hate bears."

They saw a dim light coming from the mouth of the cave. Thick vines hung over the wide entrance. Daylight peeked between the vines' leaves and branches.

"This way," Patrick said. They stepped toward the light.

Suddenly the vines parted. A figure— black against the bright light behind him— stepped into view. It was a boy.

Patrick stopped.

Beth gasped.

The boy's hand went to his waist and came up again. Light glinted off the blade of a knife.

Patrick gently pushed Beth behind him.

The boy was dressed in a short white tunic with blue trim. He also wore dark wool tights and tall leather boots. The outfit reminded Patrick of Robin Hood times.

"Who are you?" the boy asked.

"I'm Patrick," Patrick said, "and this is my cousin Beth."

"What are you doing here?" the boy asked.

"We don't know," Beth said.

"Come closer so I can see you better," the boy said.

"Put the knife away, and we will," Patrick said.

The boy glanced at the knife in his hand. Then he looked at Patrick and asked, "How do I know you are not going to attack me?"

"We're unarmed," Patrick said.

"Then what is she carrying?" the boy asked.

He gestured to Beth and the golden tablet.

Then the boy's eyes grew wide. "Is that the golden tablet?" he asked. He stepped forward.

Patrick and Beth backed up.

"Stay away," Patrick said.

The boy stopped. He looked at them. "Where did you get it?" he asked. "Did you steal it from the castle? Are you here to steal the rest of the treasure?"

"No!" Beth said.

"Give the golden tablet to me," the boy shouted. He took a step closer.

"Keep back," Patrick said.

"Give me the tablet," the boy said, "or I shall have to use force."

The boy came toward the cousins.

The Bats

"No!" Beth cried. She backed farther into the cave.

"Put that knife down," Patrick said. "We don't want to fight."

"Nor do I," the boy said. He took another step. "So give me that tablet."

Patrick stepped on a rock and almost tripped. It gave him an idea.

Patrick moved quickly. He bent over and scooped up the rock.

The boy crouched as if waiting for Patrick to attack.

Patrick lifted the rock.

"We jumped across hundreds of years to get that tablet," he said. "I'm not giving it to you."

The boy looked puzzled. "What did you say?" he asked. He lowered his knife a little.

That was Patrick's chance. He threw the rock up at the cave's ceiling. The rock hit something in the darkness. There came a flurry and flutter of wings.

Black bats flew down. Their screeches filled the cave.

Eeek! Eeek!

Beth screamed.

The bats flew past the boy. He dropped his knife and waved his hands to protect his head. He fell onto the ground.

Patrick grabbed the knife from the cave floor.

The bats were gone. Patrick stood with the knife in his hand.

Beth moved closer to Patrick. "What are you doing?" she asked.

The boy looked at Patrick and the knife.

He sat up slowly.

"Go on, knave," the boy said. "Do your worst to me."

"I want you to listen," Patrick said. "We're not thieves. That tablet was given to us."

"By who?" the boy asked.

"A Mongol princess," Beth answered.

The boy's eyes widened. "You said you jumped across hundreds of years . . ." he said slowly. "Are you friends with John of Whittaker?" the boy asked.

"John of —?" Patrick asked.

"Mr. Whittaker?" Beth said. "Yes! He sent us!"

"I am James," the boy said. "I have been writing and sending the letters to John of Whittaker."

"Why didn't you say so?" Patrick asked. He stretched out a hand to the boy.

James took Patrick's hand. Then Patrick helped the boy to his feet.

James dusted himself off. "I brought the notes to this cave. To that rock," he said.

He pointed to a flat rock. It stuck up like a small table. "John of Whittaker took the letters using his magic," James said.

Beth laughed. "It's not magic," she said. "It's the Imagination Station."

The boy frowned. "I do not understand," he said.

"It's too hard to explain," Patrick said.

Patrick turned the knife around. He made sure the handle was facing the boy. Patrick handed the knife to James. "You can have this back," Patrick said.

Beth came forward. She held out the golden tablet. "So," she said, "this is for you."

James looked at the tablet. "No," he said. He lowered himself to one knee. "But I thank God that you brought it."

"Now Albert will be saved from going to the tower," Patrick said.

James shook his head. "Not yet," he said. "There is another treasure missing. I brought a new note to the cave today."

"Another one!" Beth said.

James reached inside his tunic. He took out a rolled-up piece of paper. He handed it to Patrick.

"Please read this," James said.

Patrick took the yellowed paper. It looked like the first two notes. He read these words:

Please send us Cleopatra's crown. Lord Darkthorn will return very soon. Godspeed.

"Cleopatra's crown?" Beth asked. "You

mean the queen of Egypt?"

Patrick groaned and said, "How are we supposed to find that? We're *here*, not at Whit's End."

"There must be some way to call the Imagination Station," Beth said.

Patrick brightened up and asked Beth, "Did Mr. Whittaker say he left a remote control here?"

Beth brightened, too. "Yes!" she said. Then she frowned. "But where is it?"

Patrick turned to James. "Have you seen it?" he asked.

"Seen what?" James asked. He looked blank.

Patrick knew he couldn't explain. So he asked, "Have you seen anything strange that Mr. Whittaker left behind?"

James had a sudden thought. "The small

box?" he asked.

"Yes!" Beth said. "It would probably look like a small box."

"It is here," James said. He looked pleased. He walked to the wall and reached behind a rock. He brought something out.

The cousins watched.

This will fix everything, Patrick thought.

James said, "I took it to Albert. He wanted to see how it worked. So he opened it up."

"Opened it up?" Patrick asked. He was worried.

James held out his hand. Several small plastic and metal pieces were in it. Once the pieces might have been a remote control.

Patrick groaned. "Did he open it with a hammer?" he asked.

"Yes!" James said. He seemed pleased that

Patrick had guessed so well.

"This will never work!" Patrick said. He turned to Beth. "Now what are we going to do?"

The Letter

The cousins thought for a moment.

"I have an idea," Beth said. "Let's write in the note that we're here. Mr. Whittaker will know what to do."

Patrick shrugged. "We can try," he said and turned to James. "Do you have a pen—I mean a quill?"

James laughed. "In a cave?" he asked.

"What else can we write with?" Patrick asked.

"I have an idea," Beth said. "We can use

the knife to poke holes in the paper."

"Good idea," Patrick said. "Mr. Whittaker will see the letters when the light shines through the holes."

Beth turned to James. "May I please have the knife?" she asked.

James handed her the weapon.

Patrick spread the paper on the rock.

Beth poked tiny holes at the top.

We're stuck here! B and P

"Please ask John of Whittaker a question," James said as Beth poked the paper.

"What do you want to know?" Patrick asked.

"Why did he steal the treasures from us?" James asked.

Beth nearly dropped the knife. She said, "What?"

"Mr. Whittaker didn't take the treasures!"

Patrick said.

"Why do you think he took your treasures?" Beth asked. She crossed her arms. She was angry. "Your notes never accused him."

"It would be rude to write such a thing," James said. "But when John of Whittaker vanished, the treasures began to vanish too. So we worried that he took them for reasons of his own. That is why we wrote to him. We hoped he would return the treasures. And John of Whittaker did."

"You're wrong," Patrick said. "Mr. Whittaker didn't take them. He read your letters and wanted to help. So he sent us through history to bring the treasures back. That's why we're here."

Beth held up the letter. "It's done," she

said. "Now what do we do?"

"Put it on the rock," James said. He pointed to a large flat rock.

"Why there?" Patrick asked.

"That is where John of Whittaker disappeared," James said.

"So you put the letters on that rock," Beth said. "And they vanished?"

James said, "I would leave the cave. Then the letter would be gone when I came back."

Everything was making more sense to Patrick. "The letters on the rock must call the Imagination Station somehow," he said.

"Let's try it and see," Beth said. She moved toward the rock.

Beth put the note on the rock. All three children stepped back and watched.

Suddenly there came a flash of light. All

three children put up their hands. They stumbled back.

Beth thought she saw a flash of the Imagination Station. "Was that it?" Beth asked.

James was shaking with fear. "God save us," he said.

Patrick blinked a few times. As his eyes got used to the darkness again, he saw a figure lying next to the rock. It was a man in chain mail.

"The knight!" Patrick cried out.

"Sir Andrew!" James said.

The knight groaned. He struggled to sit up. Blood covered his shoulder.

James rushed over to him.

"Help me," Sir Andrew said. Then he slumped to the ground.

The Secret Room

James placed himself under the knight's arm. Then he pushed upward.

Patrick and Beth moved in to help. The three of them got Sir Andrew to his feet. He swayed.

"Take me to the secret room," Sir Andrew whispered.

"Is it far?" Patrick asked. Sir Andrew was very heavy, even with only his chain mail. Patrick was glad the knight wasn't wearing full armor.

"Stay with Sir Andrew," James said. "I shall be right back."

James disappeared into the darkness.

Patrick and Beth leaned Sir Andrew against a wall. The cousins propped him up with their shoulders.

The knight moaned.

Patrick and Beth heard a scratching sound. It came from the back of the cave. A yellow light flickered a moment later.

The cousins looked toward the light. James came back carrying a torch.

"Please hold this," James said to Beth.

Beth stepped away from Sir Andrew. She took the torch in one hand. In the other, she held the golden tablet.

James took her place at the knight's side.

"This way," James said. "Follow us."

Patrick and James half carried, half dragged Sir Andrew deeper into the cave. Beth followed.

Beth turned a corner and moved down a narrow passage. She came to a solid wall.

"It's a dead end," Beth said.

James smiled again. He reached a hand between two large stones. There was a click. Suddenly the wall moved.

"That way," James said.

Beth led the way into the secret room.

"Light the other torches," James called to Beth.

Beth saw torches hanging on the walls. She walked around the room and lit them.

James and Patrick took Sir Andrew to a bed of straw. They helped him lie down. Then Patrick and Beth knelt beside the knight.

James went to a jug lying nearby. He poured water into a clay cup. He brought it to Sir Andrew. The knight sat up halfway. He drank slowly from the cup.

"You are wounded," James said. He picked up a cloth. Then he gently cleaned a wound on Sir Andrew's shoulder.

"I fought the birds," the knight said softly. "The children got away safely."

"You must be dreaming," James said to him. "No bird could make a cut through your chain mail."

"The giant eagles got him," Patrick said to James. "He had to take off his armor to climb a cliff. Then he fought the birds to save us."

Sir Andrew rested his head against the straw. He closed his eyes.

Beth studied Sir Andrew's face. It was so like Mr. Whittaker's: the same nose, the same round chin, and the same thick hair. Except the knight's hair was dark brown, not gray.

Sir Andrew opened his eyes. "You are here in my time," he said. "Why?"

"We don't know," Beth said. "The Imagination Station brought us here."

"It is amazing," the knight said. He put a hand to a leather strap around his neck. On the strap was a gold ring. It had a picture on the top. The picture was of a knight inside a shield.

"That's a pretty ring," Beth said. "Where did you get it?"

The knight said, "This is John of Whittaker's magic ring."

The Second Ring

"A magic ring?" Patrick asked. "How did you get it?"

Beth groaned. "It's not magic!" she said.

"My brother Albert gave it to me," the knight said. "He was afraid it would be stolen."

"Why do you think it's magic?" Patrick asked.

"If I put it on my finger, I arrive wherever you are in time," the knight said.

Patrick smiled. "So that's how you do it!"

he said. "Mr. Whittaker's ring must trigger the Imagination Station."

"It is a mystery," the knight said.

Beth looked at Patrick. "Why would it make him follow us?" she asked.

Patrick shrugged. "The ring must have caused a glitch in the Imagination Station's computer," he said.

The knight coughed. James wiped some blood from the knight's neck. Sir Andrew winced.

"Tell me," Sir Andrew said. "Is that the golden tablet?"

Beth had forgotten all about it. She held it up for Sir Andrew to see.

"Yes," Beth said. "Isn't it beautiful?"

The knight smiled. "It will save my brother," he said.

"Please put it with the other treasures. Over there," James said. He pointed to something behind the cousins.

Patrick and Beth turned around. For the first time, they got a good look at the secret room.

Patrick's eyes went to a large blue shield. On it was a picture of a white rose. There were also several spears. Two swords leaned against the cave wall. A large trunk filled with clothes was in a corner.

Beth pointed. "Patrick, look!" she said. The Viking Sunstone and the silver cup sat on the wood table.

"The treasures are safe," James said.

Beth went to the table. She placed the golden tablet on it.

James put a cold, damp cloth on Sir

Andrew's head. The knight groaned.

"We must do something about the children's clothes," Sir Andrew said.

Patrick and Beth looked at each other. They were still in their clothes from the time of Kublai Khan.

"In that trunk," James said, "you will find some old clothes."

Patrick went over to the trunk. He pulled out a simple tunic, tights, and boots.

"What about me?" Beth asked.

"You will have to wear these," James said. He gave Beth a bundle.

She held up a long off-white dress with a red vest. "It's almost the right size," she said.

"I am sorry, but I do not have anything better," James said. "They were my sister's."

Sir Andrew slumped back onto the straw. He closed his eyes.

Beth crouched behind the large shield to change her clothes.

Patrick found a corner to put on his new clothes.

Soon they were both standing together again. Patrick looked as if he could have been a fifteenth-century farmer. Beth looked like a village girl going to church.

"Please help me undress Sir Andrew," James said to Patrick.

The two boys busied themselves with Sir Andrew's chain mail.

Beth thought they should have privacy. She moved toward the door and into the tunnel. She thought of the letter still lying on the rock. Should they leave it there?

In the main cave, Beth looked at the rock. The letter was still there. She picked up the letter and put it in her pocket.

Suddenly she heard a rustling sound. It came from the mouth of the cave. She saw figures on the other side of the vines.

She stepped toward the tunnel to warn Patrick, James, and Sir Andrew.

It was too late. Two men pushed through the vines into the cave.

Master Hugh

Beth was trapped.

If she moved toward the secret room, the strange men would see her. So she hid behind a big rock and watched them.

The two entered quietly. They stood in the middle of the cave. One was a normal-sized man. He had on a fine white shirt. The other man was huge—almost a giant.

Beth didn't know what to do. Maybe she could run outside. That would distract the men from the secret room.

No. The cave was narrow. The men would grab her.

The bats! She remembered how Patrick had scared them. She looked around and found a rock. But just as she picked it up, Sir Andrew groaned loudly.

The men turned their heads toward the sound. The smaller man signaled for the larger one to follow. They disappeared around the corner and into the tunnel.

Oh no!

Suddenly there were shouts echoing from the tunnel. Beth also heard grunts. Were they fighting?

A moment later, the men returned. The smaller one had a firm hold of James. The tall man held on to Patrick.

"As I thought," the smaller man said to James. "Albert stole the treasures. You hid them. I was wise to follow you here."

The man smiled. He seemed proud of himself.

"You have no right, Master Hugh," cried James.

"I am steward of Lord Darkthorn's castle," the man called Hugh said. "In that role I have every right to catch *thieves*."

"We are not thieves!" James said. "We are loyal to Lord Darkthorn."

"That is not how it looks," Hugh said. "The Sunstone, the silver cup, and the golden tablet are in your thieves' den."

Patrick grunted. He tried to pull away from the large man. But the man held him tight.

Hugh laughed. "Stop fighting, child," he

said. "Roderick here will knock your heads together."

The tall man gave a mean smile. He was missing three teeth.

The men pushed the boys through the vines. They all disappeared from sight.

Beth carefully came out from her hiding place. What was she going to do? Where would Hugh take the boys?

Then she remembered Sir Andrew. What had become of him? Hugh had said nothing about the knight.

Beth went down the tunnel. She crept quietly to the doorway. Torches still flickered in the secret room. She looked over at the bed of straw.

Sir Andrew was gone!

The Cottage

Beth looked around the secret room. Sir Andrew wasn't hiding. No one was there.

Is there another way out? she wondered. Then she thought, *Or maybe he put on the ring and jumped through time.*

Beth saw James's knife on the straw bed. She picked it up and wrapped it in a piece of cloth. She put the knife in her dress pocket. Then she crept back to the mouth of the cave. She peeked through the vines.

Hugh and his henchman still had hold of James and Patrick. The men were talking. Then Roderick nodded. He reached out with his free hand and grabbed James from Hugh. He dragged both boys away from the cave.

But Hugh turned around. He headed back toward Beth!

Beth jumped back. She hid behind the big rock again.

Hugh walked through the main cave and into the tunnel to the secret room.

Should I sneak away now? Beth wondered. She gave it some thought. She could follow Roderick and the boys. But what was Hugh up to? She decided to wait.

A few minutes later, Hugh came out of the tunnel. He was carrying a sack. She heard a rattle of the silver cup against the golden tablet.

Hugh has the treasures! Beth thought.

Hugh left the cave in a hurry.

Beth decided to follow him.

Hugh moved away from the cave and headed into the woods.

Beth hid close to the larger trees. She raced from one to another.

Hugh went deep into the woods.

Beth was afraid she would get lost. She tried to memorize what the trees looked like. But they all looked the same. She hoped she could find her way back.

The trees grew thicker. The branches and leaves blocked out the sun. Shadows covered everything. Beth had a hard time seeing Hugh.

All at once the steward stopped.

Beth moved behind a tree and peeked around its trunk.

Hugh stood at the door of a small stone cottage. It was covered with ivy. Hugh pushed the door open. He stepped inside.

Beth moved closer to the open cottage door. She could hear Hugh moving around inside. Candlelight flickered a moment later.

Beth carefully stepped up to the door. She peeked inside. A couple of wooden tables and chairs sat on a dirt floor. A basket of vegetables lay beside a wall.

Hugh stood at a table with his back to Beth. He took the treasures from the sack. He placed them on the tabletop.

Hugh stepped to one side.

Beth could now see the whole table.

It was covered with treasure! A silver necklace and a gold medal hung from a wooden rack. There was a white vase with flowers carved into the side. A large silver tray leaned against a marble statue.

A circle of gold was at the table's edge. It looked like a crown.

Cleopatra's crown! That was the stolen treasure James had talked about.

Hugh was the thief!

Hugh stepped over to the table again. He had a silver cup in each hand—both looked exactly the same. He grunted and put them down.

Then he lifted up the golden tablet in his right hand. And then he took another golden tablet in his left hand.

He seemed to compare them. Then he put

them down again. He did the same with the two Sunstones.

Beth thought, *Hugh doesn't know we sent the extra treasures back in the Imagination Station.*

The steward shook his head. He asked out loud, "Where did these come from? How can there be two?"

Then he suddenly hit his fist against the tabletop. He headed toward the door. Beth dashed around the corner of the cottage. She heard him slam the door.

The steward rushed past her. Then he headed back into the forest.

What should I do? Beth wondered. *Should I follow him?*

Then she had an idea.

She would take three of the treasures

back to Albert. Surely a castle couldn't be very hard to find. Then she would tell Albert what she'd seen at the cottage.

Beth sneaked into the little house. She picked up Hugh's sack. She put one silver cup, one Sunstone, and one golden tablet inside.

Back in the woods, she found a tall tree with a lot of branches. Beth climbed it. She went up as high as she could and looked out.

Lord Darkthorn's tower stood in the distance.

It was made of stone and was dark and frightening. Beneath it sat the castle.

She climbed down the tree, picked up the sack of treasures, and ran as fast as she could.

The Stocks

Beth got lost in the woods.

Night came fast. The old moon was nothing more than a sliver. It was covered in clouds.

Beth sat against a pine tree. She prayed and asked God to protect her from bears. And then she fell asleep.

At dawn she woke and found a path. She followed the trail downhill and out of the forest.

Before her was a beautiful valley.

Groves of rich green trees sat like islands in square fields of brown. A flock of sheep was grazing. A group of huts with thatched roofs was off to one side. On the far end of the valley sat the castle.

"Just like the fairy tales!" Beth said out loud.

Beth followed the path through the village. A rooster crowed. Cows mooed. Only the animals were awake this early.

She saw a small wood square in the middle of the village. It had holes in it where a person's legs would be locked down. She had seen pictures of something like it in history books. They were called *stocks*. They were used for punishing criminals.

The legs of two criminals were locked in the stocks.

Patrick and James!

Patrick woke when he heard Beth's footsteps.

Beth rushed toward him. Her red vest and long white dress flapped in the wind.

"Beth!" Patrick called. "Help! Get us out of here!"

"Shh," James said to him. "Someone will hear you."

The stocks were held shut by hinges and a lock. A sign in front of the stocks said, "A thief's end. Beware!"

Beth looked around. None of the villagers were close by.

"What are you doing here?" Beth asked.

"Roderick put us in the village jail," Patrick said. "But Master Hugh wanted the people in the village to see us."

"Master Hugh likes to scare the villagers,"

James said. "So Roderick locked us up here."

"It looks really uncomfortable," Beth said.

"It is!" Patrick said. "Now please get us out."

"How?" Beth asked.

"Use something to break the lock on the side of the stocks," Patrick said.

Beth studied the lock. "It's made of thick metal," she said. "I can't break it. I'd need a crowbar."

"Only the blacksmith has those," James said. He shook his head. "I wish I had my knife. It would be easy to pick that lock."

Beth smiled. She pulled the knife out of her pocket. "You mean *this* knife?" she asked.

James smiled and said, "I am pleased you have it. Sir Andrew gave me that knife."

James took the knife from Beth. He

reached around the side of the stocks. The thin knife tip slipped inside the lock.

James twisted the knife right. Nothing. He twisted the knife left. Nothing.

He flicked the knife back and forth.

Click.

The lock dropped off.

The boys were free. They all crept to the edge of the village. They hid behind stacks of hay.

"What have you been doing all this time?" Patrick asked.

Beth told how Sir Andrew had vanished from the secret room.

"He put on the ring when he heard Hugh coming," Patrick said.

Then she told how she'd followed Hugh to the cottage. She told them about the treasure.

Patrick said, "Hugh is stealing the treasure and letting Albert take the blame! That's awful!"

Beth then showed them the sack. She explained about the two cups, two Sunstones, and two golden tablets.

James said, "Now I understand. Master Hugh said that we would stay in the stocks until we answered his questions. He wanted to know where the extra treasures had come from. We did not know what he meant."

"We don't know where Sir Andrew is. So we must tell Albert," Patrick said to James. "Take us to him!"

9

Albert

James led the cousins away from the village path. He didn't want anyone to see them.

The three children sneaked through the trees. They came close to the castle. It was midmorning now.

Outside the castle walls, men rode on horseback. They galloped around a patch of land dotted with colorful tents. It looked almost like a circus.

Patrick pointed and asked, "What's that?"

James looked. "That is where we hold the tournaments," he said.

James started toward the castle entrance. Patrick and Beth were close behind.

"What kind of tournaments?" Beth asked.

"For the jousts and challenges of valor," James said. "Sir Andrew has defeated many knights on that field."

The three neared the castle gate. Beth expected the castle to have a moat. Instead, a drawbridge crossed over a dry rock bed with dead grass.

A guard stood at the stone entrance to the castle gate. He wore a metal helmet and held a spear. A sword in a sheath hung from his leather belt.

"What is your business?" the guard asked the children.

"We are on Sir Andrew's business," James said. "I am the knight's squire."

The guard eyed the children. "We want no beggars in the castle," he said.

"We are not beggars," James said.

"What is in the sack?" the guard asked.

"This is for Master Albert. Sir Andrew will be angry if you take it," James said. "Unless you want to fight him . . ."

The guard frowned. "Go on through," he ordered.

Beth gave the guard a small curtsy. "Thank you," she said.

The three children crossed the drawbridge. They came to a large courtyard. It was full of carts and animals and people going about their business. To one side was an area filled with hedges and flowers.

"This way," James said. He led them to the hedges. "I do not want Hugh to see us from a window. We will stay behind the hedges. We must crawl to the servant's door."

The three hunched down and crawled behind the hedges to a small metal door. They opened the door and went inside.

They crept down a hall. The castle floors were covered with rugs. They were in orange, red, yellow, and blue colors. Paintings of faces, Bible scenes, and battles hung on the walls.

The children went down a steep staircase. They came to a wood door. James knocked hard on it with his fist.

The door creaked open a moment later.

A man peered at them. He had long,

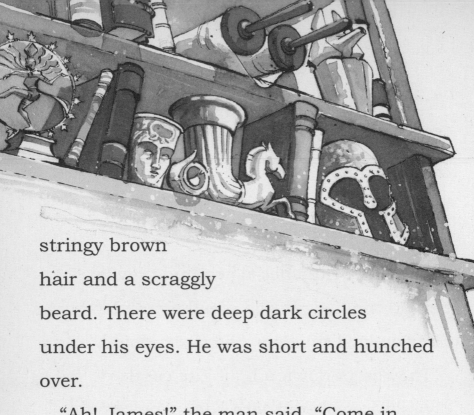

stringy brown
hair and a scraggly
beard. There were deep dark circles
under his eyes. He was short and hunched
over.

"Ah! James!" the man said. "Come in,
come in."

James and the cousins entered. The man
shut the door and bolted it.

"Who are your friends?" the man asked.

James turned to Patrick and Beth. "This
is Master Albert," he said.

Then James turned to Albert. "This is
Patrick, and Beth. They come from John

of Whittaker."

Albert led them down a short hall to a large room.

Beth's mouth fell open. The room was like a giant library and museum all in one. Shelves of books lined the walls. Tables and display cases were filled with small statues, bowls, and vases.

Albert stopped at a table in the middle of the room. The children sat around the table in wood chairs. Albert remained standing.

"Now, tell me everything," Albert said.

James explained about the treasures. He told Albert about the Imagination Station, Mr. Whittaker, and Sir Andrew.

Then Beth told Albert about Hugh, the cottage, and the stolen treasures. She put the sack on the table. But Albert didn't touch it.

Instead, the tired man kept wringing his hands. He looked very worried. Sometimes he nodded silently. Sometimes he would whisper, "Yes, yes, I see."

Then Albert said, "I don't understand how there can be two Sunstones, two silver cups, and two golden tablets."

Beth said, "Patrick and I traveled in the Imagination Station. We went to Greenland, Rome, and China. We found and sent copies of all the missing treasures to you."

Beth looked Albert in the eyes. "Where did the treasures come from in the first place?" she asked.

"Lord Darkthorn is a collector," Albert said. "He has traveled the world buying treasures. My job is to keep them safe."

Master Albert clasped his hands behind

his back. He paced around the table. "This is sad," he said. "Hugh's family has been loyal to Lord Darkthorn for many years. What is Hugh up to?"

"What can we do?" Patrick asked.

"Maybe Mr. Whittaker will send help," Beth said.

"Maybe," Patrick said. "But when? What can we do in the meantime?"

"We will stay here," James said. "Sir Andrew will come looking for us."

"Are we safe here?" Patrick asked.

"There is nowhere safer," Albert said.

Bam!

A loud sound echoed from down the hallway.

"Open this door!" a voice roared.

"That sounds like Roderick!" James said.

"Hurry!" Albert said. "You must hide!"

Caught!

The children rushed to hide. Beth sneaked behind the long curtains. Patrick crawled underneath a desk. James buried himself in a pile of old rugs.

"Now, now," Albert called. He moved down the hallway. "No need for all the noise."

Beth peeked through an opening in the curtains. She heard Albert open the door.

There were shouts. Then Hugh and Roderick rushed into the library. Albert followed them.

"Where are they?" Hugh asked. "I know the squire and his friend are in here."

Hugh nodded to Roderick. "Find them," Hugh said.

The henchman began to search the room.

"Lord Darkthorn will be unhappy to learn that you've been hiding thieves," Hugh said. He pointed a long, thin finger at Albert. "You will rot in the tower!"

Beth watched as Roderick moved around the room. He was getting close to the bag of treasures on the table. *He must not get them*, she thought.

She saw a stick on the windowsill behind her. She guessed that Albert used it to prop up the window. She picked it up and threw it to the other side of the room.

Hugh turned to look. Roderick spun round. Beth stepped back. The curtains gently moved. She hoped no one saw her.

Suddenly the red drapes were yanked aside. Roderick stood in front of her. He grabbed her arm and pulled her out.

Hugh looked shocked. "Who is this?" he asked. He looked at Albert.

Albert went pale. "She is my servant," he said.

Hugh said, "Then she will go to the tower with you!"

Roderick pulled Beth toward him. "Come!" he said.

"But I haven't done anything wrong!" Beth cried.

Just then Hugh noticed the sack on the table. "What is this?" he asked.

He picked up the end of the sack. The three treasures spilled out. First, the silver cup. Second, the Sunstone. Third, the golden tablet.

"What are these doing here?" Hugh shouted.

Roderick stopped.

"You stole them!" Beth said. "They belong here!"

Hugh's face turned red with rage. "You will suffer for this!" he shouted.

Patrick rushed into view. "No!" he cried out.

James pushed himself up from the old rugs. The knife was in his hand. "Let her go, you knave!" he shouted.

This surprised Hugh, who backed into a bookcase. Roderick stood as if waiting for orders.

Albert grabbed the sack and began

putting the treasures back inside.

Then Hugh laughed. "You are foolish," he said. Then he shouted, "Guards!"

Footsteps thudded down the hallway. Heavy footsteps. Men with spears rushed into the room.

"I think you are outnumbered," Hugh said. "And now you will go to the tower."

The Tower

Six castle guards marched Beth, Patrick, Albert, and James out of the castle. Hugh and Roderick followed them.

"What are we going to do?" Patrick whispered to Beth.

"I don't know," Beth whispered back.

They crossed a small field to the tower. The tall stone building looked scarier than ever. Beth shivered in fear.

They reached the door at the base of the

tower. Hugh took out a ring of keys from his belt. He laughed as he slid the key into the lock.

Suddenly there was a dull, heavy thudding. Was it coming from inside the tower?

No. The thudding grew louder. It came from behind them. It was the sound of a horse's hooves.

They all turned. A horse galloped toward them.

A knight in armor rode the horse. His silver armor caught the light of the sun. The armor shined brightly.

The guards grumbled. They stepped a few feet away. One of them lifted his sword.

Hugh pushed past Patrick to face the oncoming stranger.

The knight drew the horse to a stop. The

horse reared back. It was as if it didn't like Hugh.

"What goes on here, Master Hugh?" the knight called. He was talking through the visor on his helmet.

Hugh put his hands on his hips. "Who asks?" he asked.

The knight pushed the visor up to show his face. "I am Sir Andrew, as you well know," the knight said.

Patrick noticed again how much Sir Andrew looked like Mr. Whittaker. Though Sir Andrew looked pale and sick.

"This is not your concern," said Hugh. "I am dealing with these thieves. They are going in the tower."

Sir Andrew said, "Only Lord Darkthorn himself may lock people in the tower. Not his steward."

"Who are you to say what I may or may not do?" Hugh asked.

"I am a royal knight of England," Sir Andrew said. "My life is given to uphold justice. I am also a loyal follower of Lord Darkthorn. Can you say the same?"

"I defy you!" Hugh shouted.

Sir Andrew lifted his sword. "Do you challenge me, Master Hugh?" he asked.

Roderick stepped closer to Hugh. The henchman seemed fearless.

Hugh was silent, as if making up his mind. He looked at Roderick. Then he said to Sir Andrew, "Yes! I accept your challenge! We will joust on the field of valor! Prepare yourself!"

"Now?" James asked. He looked worried.

"Now," said Sir Andrew. "And let the honorable man be victorious."

Hugh nodded to Roderick. Then they turned to leave.

"What about the thieves?" one of the guards asked.

"Let Sir Andrew take them," Hugh said. "They are not to leave the castle grounds. If they escape, *he* will suffer for it."

"And Master Albert?" the guard asked.

"Take him back to his room," Hugh said.

Albert looked sadly at the children. "I'm sorry," he said.

Hugh turned on his heel. Roderick, the guards, and Albert followed him to the castle.

Beth and Patrick rushed toward Sir Andrew.

"That was a noble thing to do," Beth said. "Thank you!"

"It was the right thing to do," Sir Andrew said. He slumped forward a little in his saddle.

"Master, you are not well," James said.

"Not so," Sir Andrew said. "I've never been more ready to fight."

James asked, "But your shoulder is still hurt. How will you hold a lance?"

"As bravely as I can," said Sir Andrew. "God will see that justice is done. Hurry! We have work to do!"

The knight tugged at the reins. His horse turned around, and Sir Andrew rode away.

Beth watched Sir Andrew sway in the saddle as he rode. She was afraid.

The Tournament

Sir Andrew rode off to get his jousting weapons. James took the cousins to the tournament grounds. They would help Sir Andrew prepare for the fight.

Some men were setting up a large tent. It was at the far end of the field. The tent had a pointed roof. Small, colorful flags were attached to poles.

"What is that?" Beth asked James.

"Master Hugh is making camp there,"

James said. "The tent is where he will dress." The tent was placed at the edge of the woods. Swords, axes, clubs, and spears leaned against a rack. Horses were tied to posts in the ground.

"Where is our tent?" Beth asked.

"There is no time. We will set up camp here," James said. He pointed to an old fire pit. It was round and black with soot.

"Sir Andrew's shields will be placed on those nails," James said. He pointed to three trees nearby. Large iron spikes stuck out from the bark.

Sir Andrew arrived on his horse. The horse pulled a small wagon.

Sir Andrew wore new armor. It was bright white with blue tassels on the helmet.

James and Patrick unloaded three large

shields from the wagon. They hung them on the spikes in the trees. The blue shields were decorated with white roses.

"What does the white rose mean?" Beth asked.

"The white rose means that we are loyal to the House of York," James said. "The Duke of York should be the rightful king."

"Should be? You mean he isn't?" asked Beth.

"No," James said. "Our enemies lie about the king's claim to the throne. The king is with the House of Lancaster. Their color is red. Their shield symbol is a lion or a red rose."

It didn't make sense to Beth. She was glad America didn't have kings and queens.

James and Patrick unloaded three long lances from the wagon.

Suddenly there was cheering from the other camp. Beth looked up. Master Hugh arrived on a black horse. Roderick walked ahead of it.

Hugh was dressed in his white shirt and dark tunic. He waved to the people in his camp. Then he turned to Sir Andrew. He scowled.

Roderick helped Hugh off the horse. They went into the tent together.

"We must pray!" Sir Andrew called out. He stayed on his horse. The three children knelt.

Beth clasped her hands and closed her eyes.

"To the glory of God, the honor of Lord Darkthorn, and the rise of the Duke of York," Sir Andrew said.

Beth prayed that Sir Andrew would have the strength to fight.

The blast of a horn got their attention. A man with a long trumpet blew on the horn three times.

"Here comes the herald," said James.

A second man walked to the center of the field. The herald wore a long smock. He said loudly, "Sir Andrew and Master Hugh will now take their places!"

The gathering crowd cheered.

Sir Andrew stretched out his right hand. James gave him a lance. Patrick handed him a shield. Sir Andrew took it with his left hand.

The knight gave his horse a gentle kick. He rode to the jousting field.

Hugh came out of his tent a moment later. He wore black and red armor. His visor was down. He looked evil. Beth shivered.

It took several servants to lift the Red Knight onto his horse. The servants handed him his shield and lance.

James gasped and said, "Look! His shield is red. It has a lion on it! He is with the House of Lancaster."

"The knave is now open about being a traitor," Sir Andrew said. "He has been stealing the treasures to sell. He means to overthrow Lord Darkthorn and take over the castle."

The Red Knight trotted his horse out to the herald. The two knights on horseback faced each other. The herald was between them.

"I remind you of the rules for this joust of peace," the herald said to the two knights.

"What's a joust of peace?" Patrick asked.

James said, "A joust of peace is finished

when a knight is knocked off his horse. No one should get hurt or trampled."

The two knights turned their horses around. They rode to opposite ends of the field.

They waited. Beth had a sick feeling in her stomach.

The trumpeter blew his horn.

The two men spurred their horses forward. With growing speed, they raced toward each other. They held their lances level.

Crack!

The Red Knight's lance shattered against Sir Andrew's shield.

Sir Andrew tilted backward from the hit, but he didn't fall.

The crowd cried out. Beth winced. She knew Sir Andrew must be in great pain.

Sir Andrew rode his horse to the end of the field. Beth thought he slumped a little.

Could Sir Andrew take another hard hit?

The Red Knight took up a new lance. He got into position. He sat straight and tall.

The trumpet blew. The horses took off. The two knights came at each other.

Crack!

The two lances slammed against the shields. Both lances shattered.

The White Knight swayed. He fell forward onto his horse's neck.

The Red Knight swayed and leaned sideways. His horse galloped on. The Red Knight tilted to the left. Then he tilted to the right. Then he fell from his horse. He hit the ground.

"It's over!" Beth cried. "Sir Andrew won!"

"Wait," James said. "Something's wrong."

The Red Knight stood up slowly. He took a few steps to his horse. He pulled a long sword from the saddle. "Now we fight man to man, sword to sword!" he shouted.

Sir Andrew rode close to the Red Knight. "Follow the code of honor," Sir Andrew said. "This is a joust of peace."

"There is no peace!" the Red Knight shouted. "This is war! Lancaster against York! To the death!"

The Trick

The Red Knight swung his sword around. Sir Andrew leaned back and fell off his horse. He hit the ground on his back.

The Red Knight came forward. He swung his sword down. It hit the side of Sir Andrew's helmet.

"Not fair," James shouted. "He has no weapon!"

Sir Andrew lay still for a moment. The Red Knight brought his sword up with both hands. The sword pointed down.

"No!" Beth shouted.

Just then Sir Andrew's horse whinnied. It gave the Red Knight a hard kick.

The Red Knight stumbled to one side. He fell broadside into his own horse. Then it seemed as if he had a new idea. He took the horse's reins and hurried toward his camp.

Sir Andrew struggled to his feet. But the effort was too much. He fell to the ground again.

James rushed to his side. He carried a sword. He tried to help Sir Andrew up. But the weight was too much for him.

Patrick watched the Red Knight. The knight grabbed a new lance from one of his servants. Patrick now knew what the Red Knight was going to do. He would race toward Sir Andrew.

He would kill him with the lance. Or he would trample him with the horse.

Patrick called to Beth, "Help me!"

Patrick grabbed Sir Andrew's shield and tried to lift it. Beth ran to Patrick's side and helped.

The White Knight groaned. He struggled to rise. James was trying to push Sir Andrew upright.

The Red Knight came galloping on his horse. The lance was pointed straight for Sir Andrew.

Beth and Patrick were carrying the shield. They raced past Sir Andrew and James.

They put the shield on the ground. The cousins crouched behind the shield. They were now standing between Sir Andrew and the Red Knight.

The Red Knight came at them full speed. He couldn't have stopped the horse if he had wanted to.

Beth and Patrick braced themselves behind the shield. The loud thumping of the horse's hooves came closer. Then the lance smashed against the shield.

The blow jolted the cousins like a bolt of lightning. They fell backward. The shield landed on top of them.

The sound of the hooves stopped.

Beth peeked out from behind the shield.

The Red Knight had fallen. His helmet had been knocked off his head.

"This is trickery!" James called to the cousins. His voice was hot with anger. "The Red Knight is not Master Hugh!"

The Red Knight was stunned. He sat up.

Everyone could see that the knight was Roderick.

The crowd roared angrily.

Roderick groaned and fell back again.

"Then where is Master Hugh?" Beth asked.

"He must be hiding in his tent," James said.

He turned to Beth and Patrick. "Go back to the cave," he said. "Keep safe. Master Hugh will not give up easily. He may try to harm you. Hurry!"

"What about you?" Patrick asked.

"I will help Sir Andrew," James said. "A squire never leaves his knight."

Beth looked up. The crowd of people was rushing toward Hugh's tent.

Hugh's servants fought to keep them out.

"Capture the traitor!" some men shouted. "Get Hugh!"

Suddenly a cry rose up, "Those for Lancaster—fight now! It's our chance to take Lord Darkthorn's castle!"

"This is dangerous," James said to the cousins. He looked worried.

The crowd attacked each other with fists and sticks. Some grabbed the Red Knight's lances, battle-axes, and swords.

The children looked at Sir Andrew. He moaned and tried to sit up.

"You are not safe here! The fighting will not stop until there is death," Sir Andrew said to the cousins. "Run to the cave!"

Victory?

Beth and Patrick ran for the cave.

Beth worried about Sir Andrew. "Will the good side win?" Beth asked.

"I hope so," Patrick said.

"I think Hugh will go to the stone cottage," Beth said.

"They'll find him," Patrick said. "Roderick will lead them to it."

Beth sighed and said, "And Albert won't go into the tower."

They sat at the mouth of the cave and waited. Dark clouds rolled in.

"It's going to rain," Beth said.

Sir Andrew and James arrived an hour later. Albert was with them. They explained that Roderick confessed to everything.

Roderick told them that Hugh had been stealing treasures from Lord Darkthorn. The steward wanted to raise money for the House of Lancaster. Hugh then let Albert take the blame for the missing treasures.

Roderick led the local sheriff and several villagers to the cottage to claim the rest of the stolen treasures.

Hugh was still missing. But Sir Andrew was sure he would be caught. He would face justice when Lord Darkthorn returned.

"He will be locked in the tower," said the

knight.

Albert laughed with joy.

Sir Andrew and James went inside the secret room. Sir Andrew came out again, and he was wearing "normal" clothes.

Beth and Patrick turned to each other. Their mission was finally finished.

The Ring

It was time for the cousins to take the ring back to Mr. Whittaker.

"Can I have the ring?" Patrick asked. "If I put it on, it will summon the Imagination Station."

"I will give it to you now," Sir Andrew said.

"Wait!" Beth said. "We haven't said good-bye."

Beth hugged James, who blushed. Then she hugged Sir Andrew. Then Albert. He

chuckled warmly. His laugh also reminded the cousins of Mr. Whittaker.

Patrick didn't give any hugs. But he shook their hands. He found it hard to say anything.

"We are forever grateful to you," Sir Andrew said.

"Maybe we'll see you again sometime," Beth said.

"Let's go," Patrick said to Beth.

Sir Andrew took the ring off his leather strap.

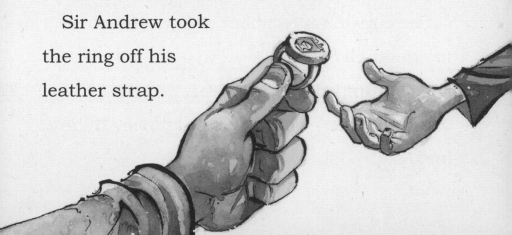

He held it out to Patrick.

The ring was within an inch of Patrick's finger. Then something surprising happened.

Master Hugh rushed forward out of the shadows. He snatched the ring from Sir Andrew's hand.

"Fools!" Hugh shouted. He put the ring on his own finger.

The Imagination Station appeared. Hugh laughed and leaped into the machine.

"Oh no!" Beth said.

"The knave!" James said.

"After him!" Patrick shouted.

The cousins scrambled toward the Imagination Station.

They jumped in. They searched the machine. They were afraid Hugh was hiding inside.

But he wasn't there.

The door closed shut.

"Where is he?" Beth asked.

"Remember? This happened before with Sir Andrew," Patrick said. "He got into the Imagination Station. But he disappeared when we followed him."

"So where did Hugh go? Will he be back at Whit's End?" asked Beth.

"There's only one way to find out," Patrick said. He reached forward and pushed the red button.

16

The Workshop

Mr. Whittaker was waiting at Whit's End. Beth and Patrick stepped out of the Imagination Station.

"Something went wrong," Mr. Whittaker said. There was a deep worry line between his eyebrows.

"Master Hugh took your ring," Patrick said. "He got into the Imagination Station. Is he here?"

Mr. Whittaker shook his head. "No. But

who is Master Hugh?" he asked.

"He's the bad guy," Beth said.

The cousins took turns telling Mr. Whittaker all that had happened.

"So, my ring made it possible to travel," Mr. Whittaker said softly. "That explains a lot."

"It does?" Beth said. "How?"

Mr. Whittaker paced around the machine. "The Imagination Station must have been confused about the ring," he said. "It thinks that whoever is wearing it is me. That's why it wouldn't work for me. It thinks I'm in there somewhere."

"But Hugh has it now. And we don't know where he is!" Patrick said.

Mr. Whittaker nodded. "Now that I know the ring is the problem, I can try to track where it is."

"You'd better hurry," Patrick said.

"Hugh is a mean and selfish man," Beth added. "He could cause all kinds of trouble in history."

"I'll create a program to find him," Mr. Whittaker said. "We have to get him back to his right time."

"But how? *You* can't do it," Patrick said.

"I'll figure it out," Mr. Whittaker said.

Patrick and Beth looked at each other knowingly.

Mr. Whittaker went to work on the Imagination Station computer.

There was nothing else to say. The cousins gathered their things to go home.

Mr. Whittaker looked at them from the computer keyboard. "Patrick, Beth, thank you for everything you've done," he said warmly. "I'm truly grateful."

"You're welcome," the cousins said. "We had some wonderful adventures."

Patrick leaned toward Beth. He whispered, "And I think we're going to have a few more."

Secret Word Puzzle

Patrick and Beth wanted to find out who was stealing the treasures in *Revenge of the Red Knight.* Now you can solve a mystery too—and find the secret word.

Below is a number/letter code. A = 1, B = 2, C = 3, and so on. Use the code to fill in the correct letters above the numbers. Then fill in the answer to the code. Write the answer inside the boxes to know the secret word.

A = 1	H = 8	O = 15	V = 22
B = 2	I = 9	P = 16	W = 23
C = 3	J = 10	Q = 17	X = 24
D = 4	K = 11	R = 18	Y = 25
E = 5	L = 12	S = 19	Z = 26
F = 6	M = 13	T = 20	
G = 7	N = 14	U = 21	

$$\overline{20}\ \overline{8}\ \overline{5}\quad\quad \overline{14}\ \overline{1}\ \overline{13}\ \overline{5}\quad\quad \overline{15}\ \overline{6}\quad\quad \overline{20}\ \overline{8}\ \overline{5}$$

$$\overline{13}\ \overline{1}\ \overline{4}\quad\quad \overline{23}\ \overline{5}\ \overline{1}\ \overline{18}\ \overline{9}\ \overline{14}\ \overline{7}\quad\quad \overline{20}\ \overline{8}\ \overline{5}$$

$$\overline{18}\ \overline{5}\ \overline{4}\quad\quad \overline{1}\ \overline{18}\ \overline{13}\ \overline{15}\ \overline{18}\quad\quad \overline{9}\ \overline{19}$$

▢ ▢ ▢ ▢ ▢ ▢ ▢ ▢

(see pages 92–93)

Go to **TheImaginationStation.com**
Look for the cover of this book
and click on "Secret Word."
Type in the correct answer,
and you'll receive a prize.

FOCUS ON THE FAMILY®

No matter who you are, what you're going through, or what challenges your family may be facing, we're here to help. With practical resources —like our toll-free Family Help Line, counseling, and Web sites— we're committed to providing trustworthy, biblical guidance, and support.

Focus on the Family Clubhouse Jr.

Creative stories, fascinating articles, puzzles, craft ideas, and more are packed into each issue of *Focus on the Family Clubhouse Jr.*® magazine. You'll love the way this bright and colorful magazine reinforces biblical values and helps boys and girls (ages 3–7) explore their world. **Subscribe now at Clubhousejr.com.**

Focus on the Family Clubhouse

Through an appealing combination of encouraging content and entertaining activities, *Focus on the Family Clubhouse*® magazine (ages 8–12) will help your children—or kids you care about—develop a strong Christian foundation. **Subscribe now at Clubhousemagazine.com.**

AUTHOR MARIANNE HERING
is former editor of *Focus on the Family Clubhouse*® magazine. She has written more than a dozen children's books. She likes to take walks in the rain with her golden retriever, Chase.

ILLUSTRATOR DAVID HOHN
draws and paints books, posters, and projects of all kinds. He works from his studio in Portland, Oregon.

AUTHOR PAUL McCUSKER
is a writer and director for *Adventures in Odyssey*®. He has written over fifty novels and dramas. Paul likes peanut butter-and-banana sandwiches and wears his belt backward.